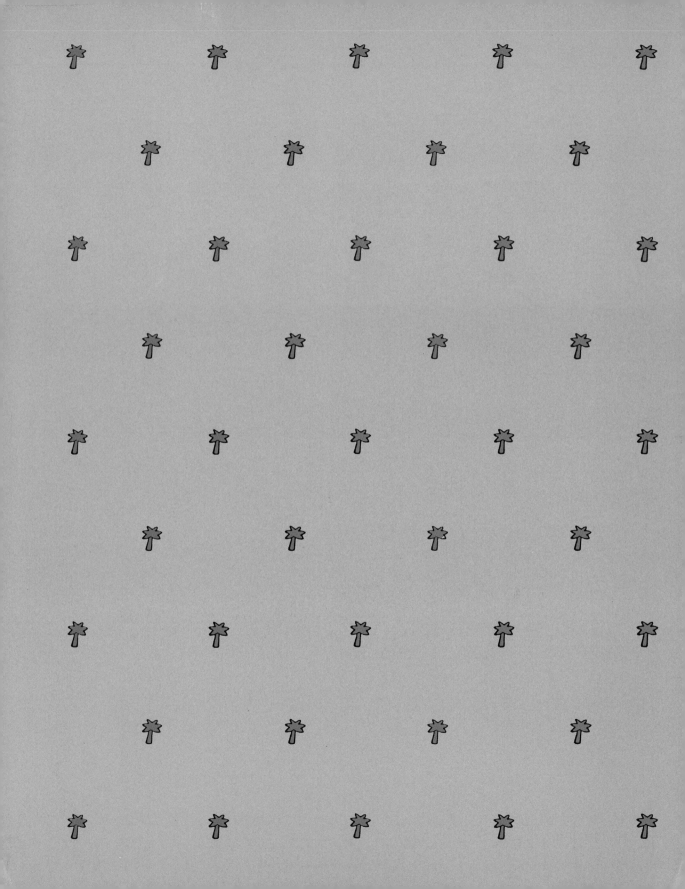

Carnival

by Denise Burden-Patmon
with Kathryn D. Jones

Illustrated by
Reynold Ruffins

MULTICULTURAL CELEBRATIONS

MODERN CURRICULUM PRESS

Multicultural Celebrations was created under the auspices of
 The Children's Museum, Boston.
Leslie Swartz, Director of Teacher Services,
organized and directed this project with
funding from The Hitachi Foundation.

Design: Gary Fujiwara
Photographs: *10, 13, 21,* Leslie Swartz.

 MODERN CURRICULUM PRESS, INC.
13900 Prospect Road
Cleveland, Ohio 44136

ISBN 0-8136-2274-3 (soft cover)   0-8136-2275-1 (hard cover)
5 6 7 8 9 10   95 94 93
Simon & Schuster   A Paramount Communications Company

The sound of the *calypso* beat was sweet—oh,
so sweet. Rosa sat straight up in bed—was she
dreaming? Could it be true?

There it was again. She jumped out of bed and
ran to the window.

"When I pull up the shade, the white sands and blue water of home will stretch out in front of me," she whispered.

The shade rolled up, but there was no white sand and no beautiful, blue water. Rosa saw only tall buildings, with cars and buses swoosh, swooshing on busy streets.

"Oh, why did I have to come to Brooklyn anyway?" Rosa thought as she tugged on her jeans. "Aunt Leila and Uncle Cecil are okay, but I miss Trinidad . . . and my dad . . . and my friends . . ."

Then she heard the drum again. Rosa just had to find out where it was coming from. As she ran past Claude's room, she heard him call out, "Hey, where are you going so fast?"

Rosa scowled as she headed for Aunt Leila's kitchen. She was getting really tired of her older cousins trying to make her like New York. She hated the city noise. She missed the gentle island sounds.

"I know I promised Dad I would try to make the best of this move, but . . . " Rosa mumbled to herself. She sniffed the air. What was that smell? *Hot roti*? *Channa*? *Saltfish cakes*? Now she was really homesick.

"There you are, sweetheart," said Aunt Leila, giving Rosa a hug. "I was wondering if you were going to sleep through *Carnival*!"

"I still can't get used to celebrating *Carnival* in September, Aunt Leila. Things sure are different here in Brooklyn."

"Oh—there I go, forgetting this is all new to you," said her aunt. "We celebrate *Carnival* over Labor Day weekend because it's too cold to do it in March or April," she said laughing. "All of us from the Caribbean get together to have our own special celebration."

"It's like the *Carnival* I remember in Barbados," said Uncle Cecil as he came in. "Leila, can you get the food out to the stand? I have to meet everyone at the warehouse to get ready for the parade."

6

Parade! Rosa could hardly believe it. Maybe things were looking up after all.

"Well, the boys can help carry the food," Aunt Leila said as she poured curried goat into the big pots. "And Rosa can . . . "

"Wait a minute, I don't have much time," said Claude, grabbing an orange on his way through the kitchen.

"I'll help you carry the food, but I can't stay at the stand," said Luther, coming in last. "I have to meet my friends, too."

"That's fine," Leila answered. "Just be sure to take Rosa with you."

"Rosa? She never wants to do anything but dream about Trinidad. She's not even trying to get used to Brooklyn."

"Boys, help your mother. Never mind about Rosa," Uncle Cecil interrupted. "I have something special in mind for her. Let's get going, honey."

Uncle Cecil and Rosa headed down Eastern Parkway. It was already crowded with people in masks and costumes, and groups setting up food stands. Rosa spotted a *steel band*.

"I knew I heard a *pan* this morning. I thought I was dreaming!" Rosa exclaimed.

"No it wasn't a dream, Rosa. The *calypso* musicians are warming up for the parade," Cecil answered. "Some are from Trinidad—some from Barbados. You see, all the islands will be in the *Mas* parade. Looking real sharp there, Rufus," Uncle Cecil called to a tall man in a brightly-colored costume. "What a great mask!"

Rosa began to feel a little better as they walked through the crowds. They stopped at a stand to buy sweet bread and cool glasses of *mawby*. Everywhere people were smiling and friendly to them, but Rosa still felt like something wasn't quite right. It wasn't home.

"If I were back home, *I'd* be in the parade. I'd . . ."

"Now we've got to get to the warehouse," Uncle
Cecil interrupted. "We're late already."

"Can I wait for you here?" asked Rosa, not wanting
to leave the excitement of the *Carnival* in the street.

"I have a special job for you. I wrote to your dad
that *Carnival* time here was coming. He wrote back
that you have a very interesting talent that I might be
able to use."

Curious, Rosa followed him into a huge building
around the corner. She couldn't believe her eyes.
It was like a *Carnival* wonderland—everywhere
there were floats and people in costumes—it was a
sea of sequins, mirrors, feathers, horns, and crowns.
There was even a *Moko Jumbie* on stilts!

14

"Look, I bet those two will win the King and Queen competition," Uncle Cecil said, pointing to a pair dressed in colorful costumes. "And here, I have something just for you," he said, handing Rosa a square box tied with string.

"For me?" Rosa asked, opening it. She pulled out a bright blue T-shirt. "But . . . "

"Now, do you see that *steel band* over there on the platform?" Rosa looked across at the group all dressed in bright blue T-shirts.

"They're ready to join the parade, but I happen to know they need one more person to play bass *pan*. Do you know anybody who could help them out?"

Rosa's face broke into a wide smile.

Soon it was noon and the glittering parade began.
The music—the floats—the cheering crowds—all
enjoying the late summer sun.

"Aunt Leila! Claude! Over here!" shouted Rosa as
they passed. "It's me—Rosa! Come on along.
Celebrate *Mas!*"

Glossary

calypso (kuh-LIP-soh) the traditional music of Carnival, from the West Indies

Carnival (KAR-nuh-vuhl) a festival with parades, costumes, and music which is celebrated at different times of the year in different countries—in Trinidad (Rosa's birthplace), it is held in March or April, several weeks before Easter; in colder climates in North America, Carnival is often held at the end of summer

channa (CHAHN-uh) seasoned chick peas

hot roti (HAHT ROH-tee) large, flat, round bread, which is sometimes filled with vegetables and meats, and eaten like a sandwich

Mas (MAHS) a word from Trinidad meaning anything to do with Carnival

mawby (MORE-bee) a drink made from tree bark with spices and sugar

Moko Jumbie (MOH-koh JUM-bee) a stilt walker who sometimes represents a ghost, a spirit, or a healer-magician

pan (PAN) another word for a steel drum made from a large empty oil drum

saltfish cakes (SALT-fish KAYKS) a dish made of salted fish mixed with potatoes or bread crumbs, and fried

steel band (STEEL BAND) a group of musicians who play drums that are made from big empty oil drums

22

About the Authors

Denise Burden-Patmon teaches at Wheelock College in Boston, Massachusetts. She has written widely on multicultural education, curriculum development, and teaching writing to children. This book is dedicated to her mother, who taught her to celebrate her African-American roots.

A native of Roxbury, Massachusetts, **Kathryn D. Jones** has lived and studied in Guyana. Since 1985 she has worked at The Children's Museum, Boston. She recently received a degree in English and Elementary Education from the University of Massachusetts at Boston.

About the Illustrator

Reynold Ruffins attended Cooper Union in New York City and has won awards from the Society of Illustrators and the Art Directors Club. He and Jane Sarnoff have written and illustrated many children's books including *A Great Bicycle Book, The Chess Book,* and *The Monster Riddle Book.*